Jessie
the Lyrics
Fairy

To Madeleine and Jude Boddice with lots of love

ORCHARD BOOKS
338 Euston Road, London NW1 3BH
Orchard Books Australia
Level 17/207 Kent Street, Sydney, NSW 2000
A Paperback Original

First published in 2012 by Orchard Books

HiT entertainment

A CIP catalogue record for this book is available
from the British Library.

ISBN 978 1 40831 5897

1 3 5 7 9 10 8 6 4 2

Printed in Great Britain

The paper and board used in this paperback are natural recyclable
products made from wood grown in sustainable forests. The
manufacturing processes conform to the environmental regulations
of the country of origin.

Orchard Books is a division of Hachette Children's Books,
an Hachette UK company

www.hachette.co.uk

Jessie
the Lyrics
Fairy

by Daisy Meadows

ORCHARD

www.rainbowmagic.co.uk

Jack Frost's Spell

It's high time for the world to see
The legend I was born to be.
The prince of pop, a dazzling star
My fans will flock from near and far.

But pop star fame is hard to get
Unless I help myself, I bet.
I need a plan, a cunning trick
To make my stage act super-slick.

Seven magic clefs I'll steal
They'll give me pop star powers, I feel.
I'll sing and dance, I'll dazzle and shine
And pop star glory will be mine!

Contents

Off to the Island

"Rainspell Island, here we come!" cheered Kirsty Tate, pointing ahead to the green island which had just appeared in view. She and her best friend Rachel Walker were on the deck of a ferry, heading off to the island, which was a very special place. Not only was it where the girls had first met, it was also the place where they'd had their very first fairy adventure.

"Nearly there," said Rachel. "I can't wait to see The Angels again, can you?"

"It's going to be awesome," Kirsty replied. The Angels were the girls' favourite band, and were performing at the five-day Rainspell Island Music Festival. Kirsty and Rachel were going to camp at the festival with Rachel's parents.

"Music, fashion, fun… We're going to have the best time ever," Rachel smiled.

"And what would make it even better," Kirsty said, lowering her voice, "is if we could meet some new fairies too." The girls exchanged a secret smile.

It was thanks to the fairies, really, that they were here at all. One Christmas, they'd won a competition to meet The Angels and had ended up helping Destiny the Pop Star Fairy to find her missing magical objects. To thank the girls for their help in making their Christmas concert a success, The Angels had invited them to the summer music festival as their special guests.

"We will shortly be arriving at Rainspell Island," came a voice over the tannoy just then. "Thank you for travelling with us today."

The island was really close now, and the girls could see a huge stage in one of Rainspell's lush green fields. There were tents and marquees and camper vans everywhere, some flying colourful flags.

11

"That must be the festival!" Rachel said excitedly. "Oh, I have such a good feeling about this, Kirsty. I know we're going to have a brilliant time!"

The girls left the ferry with Mr and Mrs Walker and made their way towards the bustling festival site. They could hear loud music and smell hot dogs, frying onions and candy floss. Then Kirsty gasped. "There are The Angels!" she cried. "Look – they're over by the main entrance!"

There was a long queue to get into the site but as soon as the three Angels spotted Kirsty and Rachel they waved them over. "Hey – welcome to Rainspell!" smiled Serena. "It's good to see you again."

"You too," the two friends chorused.

"We have your backstage passes here," Lexy said, holding up laminated passes on pink ribbons. "With these, you'll be able to skip the queue and go straight in with us."

"We can show you Star Village if you like?" Emilia suggested. "There's lots going on there, it's really cool."

"Thank you, that's very kind," Mrs Walker said, looping her pass around her neck. She looked almost as excited as the girls, Rachel noticed with a grin.

Together, they walked to Star Village, which was a collection of tents where you could try all sorts  of fun stuff: learn musical instruments and dance routines, experiment with hair and make-up, even design funky costumes just like real pop stars.

"We'll leave you to it," Emilia said after a while. "We need to do our sound check now."

"The campsite is the next field along when you want to set up," Serena said, noticing the bulky tent bag that Mr Walker was carrying.

"I hope you'll come and see us on stage later on," Lexy added. "We're opening the festival this afternoon."

To the girls' delight, the three singers broke into one of their greatest hits, *Key to My Heart*, and sang the chorus in harmony:

"You're always there to hold my hand,
You stand by me, you understand.
When I'm with you I feel so glad,
The truest friend I ever had.
I know we two will never part,
And that's the real key to my heart!"

"I love that song," Kirsty smiled. "It makes me think about being best friends with Rachel."

"Me too!" Rachel said.

The Angels high-fived them. "That's great," Lexy said. "See you later, girls!"

Kirsty and Rachel beamed as the band walked away. "I can't believe we're actually friends with The Angels, Rachel," Kirsty sighed. "They are *so* cool!"

"I know," Rachel said dreamily. "It's nearly as amazing as being friends with the fairies," she added in a whisper. "We're definitely the luckiest girls in the world!"

A Meeting with Destiny

When they reached the campsite, Kirsty and Rachel helped Mr and Mrs Walker put up the tent. The girls would be sharing one of the sleeping areas so they blew up their airbeds and unrolled their sleeping bags. It was going to be cosy in there at night, Kirsty thought, putting her pyjamas under her pillow with a smile.

Rachel's parents were just hammering in the last tent pegs when Rachel spotted a sparkly piece of material at the bottom of the tent bag. "What's this?" she asked, picking it up.

"It's a flag I brought to fly from the top of the tent," her dad replied. "It's so colourful, it'll make it easy for you girls to see it through the crowds and find your way back to the tent."

"Cool," said Rachel, unrolling the flag. But as she did so, something glittery fell out... and then soared up into the air.

It was Destiny the Pop
Star Fairy!

Kirsty waved
excitedly at
their pretty
fairy friend,
not daring
to speak
in case
Rachel's
parents
overheard.
The girls knew
that they had to keep the fairies secret
from anyone else.

She and Rachel beckoned Destiny to
follow them around the back of the tent
where they could talk without having to
worry about being overheard.

"Hello!" Kirsty said. "What a nice surprise. Have you come to hang out with the human pop stars here?"

Destiny smiled. Her magic made sure that pop concerts went perfectly in the human world as well as in Fairyland. "I'll be popping in and out," she replied, "because the Fairyland Music Festival starts today too. In fact, I was wondering if you two would like to come to Fairyland with me, and watch the rehearsal?"

"Yes, please!" Rachel said at once. Her heart gave a thump at the thought of going back to Fairyland. It was the most exciting place ever.

Even better, time stood still in the human world while they were in Fairyland, so nobody would know the girls had been gone.

"I hoped you'd say that," Destiny grinned, and waved her wand. A fountain of fizzing, sparkling fairy dust poured from its tip and swirled all around the girls. In the blink of an eye, they were whisked off the ground. Everything blurred before them in a whirlwind of dazzling rainbow colours.

When the glittery whirlwind finally
cleared, Rachel and Kirsty found
themselves in a Fairyland meadow –
and they were fairies! Kirsty couldn't
resist fluttering her wings and floating
up into the air. Being able to fly was
so wonderful!

"Oh wow, is that a fairy campsite?"
Rachel asked, gazing at the field in front
of them. They could see lots of colourful
toadstool-shaped huts and tents.

"I bet that's Danielle the Daisy Fairy's tent," Kirsty said with a giggle, pointing to a tent with a colourful pattern of yellow and white flowers on it.

"Yes, this is the camping area at our festival," Destiny said, fluttering into the air. "Let's see how everyone's getting on backstage."

Kirsty and Rachel flew after their friend, looking down at the festival site with great interest. They could see the Music Fairies setting up their instruments on stage, the Showtime Fairies checking the lights and sound system, and even the Petal Fairies, decorating the equipment with looping garlands of colourful flowers. Everyone seemed very excited.

Backstage, Destiny headed straight for a group of seven fairies who were deep in conversation. "Kirsty, Rachel, these are my very good friends the Pop Star Fairies," she said, and introduced them all. There was Jessie the Lyrics Fairy, Adele the Singing Coach Fairy, Vanessa the Dance Steps Fairy, Miley the Stylist Fairy, Frankie the Make-up Fairy, Rochelle the Star Spotter Fairy and Una the Concert Fairy.

27

To Kirsty's surprise, the Pop Star Fairies seemed rather distracted. "Hi," they said, but their smiles didn't last long. Perhaps they were just nervous about performing, she thought.

"Good luck, girls, I'm sure the rehearsal will be fine," Destiny said breezily. "Let's take our seats in the audience," she added to Rachel

and Kirsty. As the girls turned to leave, Rachel couldn't help noticing that the Pop Star Fairies immediately huddled together and began whispering anxiously.

"We'll just have to hope for the best,"
she heard Jessie say. How strange!

Destiny led them

to some seats

near Queen

Titania

and King

Oberon,

who

waved

and

smiled.

A cheerful pop tune started playing, and
on came the Pop Star Fairies to begin
the rehearsal!

Rachel listened eagerly. Fairy pop
music was sure to be awesome! But then
the fairies started singing, and almost
immediately she changed her mind.

"Oh dear," Kirsty murmured, as Una and Jessie both forgot the lyrics of the first verse.

"Ooops," Rachel whispered, wincing as Vanessa and Rochelle got their dance routine wrong and bumped into each other.

Frankie's dangly earrings fell out and Adele's dress ripped… and *all* of them were singing out of tune.

Destiny looked horrified. "This is a disaster!" she whispered.

"What's going wrong?" Kirsty hissed. She was sure the Pop Star Fairies weren't usually this bad.

"I think they must have forgotten their clefs," Destiny whispered back. "A clef is a symbol used for writing music down, and all the Pop Star Fairies have magical clef necklaces. Wearing them makes sure that pop music is wonderful in your world and in ours. Without them, pop performances can go very wrong  – like this one." She scratched her head. "But I don't understand. They *always* wear their magical clefs.

How could they have forgotten today?"

Rachel's heart sank. "So without their clefs, pop performances in the human world will go wrong too?" she realised. "I hope they remember to put them back on soon!"

Just then, a cold breeze swept through the audience. Icicles appeared around the stage, as well as a white layer of frost on the ground. Kirsty felt goosebumps  prickle across her arms and glanced at Rachel in alarm. "Oh no – is Jack Frost here?" she gulped.

Before anyone could reply, Jack Frost
and his goblin servants strutted on stage.
Jack Frost was dressed like a rock star,
and Destiny gasped in dismay as she
saw that seven necklaces were hanging
around his neck, each with a different
colour musical clef on it.

"Oh no,"
she wailed.
"So the
Pop Star
Fairies didn't
forget their
magical
clefs. Jack
Frost must
have stolen
them!"

Memory Mayhem!

Queen Titania had also noticed that Jack Frost was wearing the magical clef necklaces and rose to her feet. "Those don't belong to you," she called out. "Give them back to the Pop Star Fairies."

A sly smile appeared on Jack Frost's cold, pointy face. "No way," he said. "Not now that I know what these do."

He played a series of melodic chords on his guitar, the notes ringing out perfectly around the stage. The goblins clapped, and Jack Frost bowed.

"I've definitely got the Frost Factor," he cackled, "and what's more, I'm going to use these magical clefs to make me the biggest star that the

Rainspell Island Music Festival has ever seen. Nothing's going to stop me now!"

A flash of blue icy magic lit up the stage and before anyone could react, Jack Frost and his goblins had disappeared from view. Destiny, meanwhile, had turned pale, and all the Pop Star Fairies looked very upset.

"Your Majesties, Kirsty and I are staying at the Rainspell Island Music Festival," said Rachel. "We'll try our best to get the magical clefs back for you while we're there."

"Thank you," King Oberon replied, looking grave. "That's very kind. Jessie, perhaps you can take the girls to the human world and help them."

"Of course," said Jessie at once, jumping lightly off the stage. She had black hair and big dangly hoop earrings.

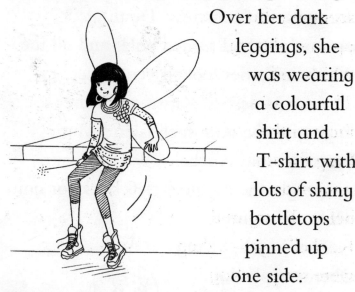

Over her dark leggings, she was wearing a colourful shirt and T-shirt with lots of shiny bottletops pinned up one side.

"Good luck," Destiny said. "And please do your best. Without those magical clefs, I'm afraid pop music is in big trouble."

"We'll try our hardest," Jessie promised. "Let's go!"

She waved her wand and a flurry of orange sparkles whizzed around the three of them, scooping them up in a glittery whirlwind. The anxious faces of their fairy friends vanished before Kirsty and Rachel's eyes as they were swept away.

Moments later they were back on Rainspell Island, still as fairies. "Let's fly around and look for Jack Frost," Jessie suggested. "But remember to stay well out of sight. There are so many people here, we mustn't let anyone see us!"

The three fairies zoomed high above
the crowds, searching for any signs of
Jack Frost or his goblins causing trouble.
They flew into the backstage area
which was a large, airy tent lined with
comfortable sofas, special practice areas
where the performers could rehearse, and
tables full of sandwiches and cakes.

Kirsty felt tingly with excitement as she spotted her favourite boy band A-OK practising their harmonies, and saw other pop stars there too. "Sasha Sharp, Groove Gang, Dakota May, Jacob Bright…" she said, pointing them out to Rachel. "Wow!"

"None of them look very happy though," Rachel said as one of the A-OK boys put his head in his hands.

Dakota May came to a stop in the middle of her song and let out a wail. "I forgot the words *again!*" she cried.

"They keep forgetting their song lyrics," Kirsty realised.

"Oh dear," Jessie groaned. "It's because Jack Frost has my clef. When I'm wearing it, it helps pop stars compose wonderful lyrics – and remember them too!"

"Look, there are The Angels," Rachel said, spotting them rehearsing in a far corner. "Let's see if they're having better luck."

Unfortunately, as they flew closer, it soon became obvious that The Angels were also struggling.

"You're always there to… make my tea…" Serena sang, then looked puzzled. "No, that's not right."

"You're always there to… hold my bags…" Emilia tried next, frowning. "What *is* that line again?"

"We've got to find my magical clef as soon as we can," Jessie said. "The Angels are meant to be opening the festival in half an hour, and they can't remember the first line of their biggest hit. This could go horribly wrong!"

"Well, there's no sign of Jack Frost in here," Kirsty said. "Let's try looking somewhere else."

The three fairies flew out of the backstage marquee and back around the festival site. There were lots of people having fun in Star Village, enjoying the sunshine and setting out picnic lunches, but no goblins or Jack Frost in sight.

Rachel was just starting to wonder if he was even at the festival at all, when she noticed a big crowd pouring into the karaoke tent. "We could try looking in there," she suggested.

Jessie and Kirsty agreed, and they flew closer. Someone inside was rapping – and as they approached the tent, the three fairies realised the same thing at the same time: the rapper's lyrics were coming out perfectly.

"He's the only person we've heard in this festival to get the words right," Jessie said. "I bet that means he's near my magical clef!"

All Change

Kirsty, Rachel and Jessie immediately flew over the heads of the crowd and into the karaoke tent to investigate. Inside, there were small karaoke booths set up with microphones and TV screens. All of the booths were empty except for one, where the rapper stood, surrounded by a huge crowd. He wore a sparkly green baseball jacket and a cap with a large visor that hid his face from view.

As he finished the rap, he bowed low, and the audience cheered.

The rapper swaggered around. "Thanks," he said into the microphone. "Glad you liked it. That was a song by Jax Tempo, my hero! He's the only rapper in the whole world who's better than me." He patted his throat. "Gotta protect this voice of mine now, so that was the last song. Later, guys!"

Rachel's eyes widened as he patted his throat and she noticed a gleam of orange beneath his fingers. Immediately she nudged her friends. "Look!" she hissed. "Have you seen what he's got around his neck?"

Jessie stared excitedly down at the rapper. "It's my clef!" she exclaimed. "Jack Frost must have split the clefs up and given them to his goblins to hide!"

"Goblins are too vain to not to use the clefs themselves!" giggled Kirsty. "But there are so many people around. How are we going to get near him without anyone seeing us?"

The three friends tried to think of a solution. "If we can somehow get him to take it off…" Jessie murmured, scratching her head.

Rachel smiled. "I've got an idea," she said. "We'll suggest that he has an image change. Like this…" And she whispered her plan to the other two.

"Let's fly into an empty booth and I'll work some magic on you two," Jessie said. "Quick," she added as the goblin gave a last wave to his fans and began heading towards the exit. "Before we lose sight of him."

The three fairies swooped down into a booth. When nobody was looking, Jessie waved her wand, releasing a sparkling stream of fairy magic. A split-second later, both Kirsty and Rachel were back to their usual size… but now they each wore a disguise. Kirsty was wearing a smart trouser suit with a badge that read 'Star Spotter' while Rachel had an official festival cap on her head, and held a clipboard in her hand.

"So you're a show-business agent, and I'm a festival organiser," Rachel giggled. "Come on, let's try it. I'll meet you backstage. Good luck!"

She hurried off, and Jessie fluttered towards one of the speakers high in the ceiling of the tent, then gave Kirsty a thumbs-up. Kirsty smiled back, took a deep breath and walked towards the goblin. She hoped this would work!

Superstar!

"Hi, I'm Crystal Gold, agent to the stars," Kirsty told the goblin. "I'm always on the lookout for amazing new talent – and I think you're it."

The goblin looked delighted and struck a pose. "Well, I *am* pretty good, it's true," he replied, boastfully.

"The Angels keep forgetting their song lyrics and the festival people are worried they won't be able to perform at their best," Kirsty went on, "so I'd like to suggest you as their replacement. What do you think – are you up to appearing on the main stage as our opening act?"

"Too right!" the goblin beamed. "At last – my chance to shine in the spotlight!"

Kirsty scratched her ear – the secret signal she'd agreed with Jessie – and saw some little orange sparkles flash above the speaker. Then a voice boomed out. "Attention, please. Could our opening act make their way to the main stage now, please? Thank you."

Clever Jessie had used fairy magic to disguise her voice so that it sounded like a tannoy announcement – and by the look of excitement on the goblin's face, it had been very convincing.

"What are we waiting for?" he whooped. "Let's go!"

57

He raced eagerly towards the main stage. Kirsty held her jacket pocket open wide so that Jessie could dive inside and hide there, then ran after him. She took the goblin to the wings of the main stage, using her backstage pass to get them both inside. As they'd planned,

Rachel was there to meet them.

"Hmm," Rachel said, looking the goblin up and down critically. "I'm not sure…"

The goblin drooped. "What do you mean?" he asked.

"I don't know if you've got the star quality we're looking for at the moment," Rachel told him. "You don't look quite right."

"He can change," Kirsty said, elbowing the goblin. "Can't you? You could wear something different."

"Yes, of course," the goblin replied, clearly desperate to get on the main stage at any cost.

"I'll do anything!"

"OK, well, the sparkly baseball jacket and the cap need to go for a start," Rachel ordered.

The goblin obediently took them off.

"And that orange necklace – it's not saying 'rap star' to me," Rachel added.

The goblin put a hand to the necklace... then seemed to change his mind. "No," he said stubbornly. "The necklace stays."

Rachel hesitated. Oh dear! That wasn't part of the plan. She was just starting to wonder what to say next when Kirsty had a stroke of genius.

"Don't you worry," Kirsty said, patting the goblin's arm. "As your new agent, I'll sort this out for you. Wait there." She dashed behind a rail of costumes and hissed to Jessie, "Please can you magic up something that the goblin will want to wear around his neck?"

Jessie grinned and leaned out of Kirsty's pocket to wave her wand.

There was a swirl of orange sparkles, and then a chunky gold chain appeared in Kirsty's hand, with a large medallion reading 'Superstar' hanging from it.

"Perfect!" Kirsty giggled, and went back to find the goblin. "Here," she said. "This will look *much* cooler than that flimsy little necklace."

The goblin's eyes lit up. "Superstar – yes, that's me!" he agreed. He grabbed the gold chain and hurled off Jessie's clef necklace at once.

Kirsty deftly caught the necklace, then passed it to Jessie who immediately shrank it down to fairy size. As Jessie fastened it around her neck and the clef shone brightly, all three friends beamed. They'd done it!

All the Fun of the Festival

The goblin, meanwhile, was practising his act and hadn't noticed any of this. Unfortunately, now that he was no longer wearing Jessie's clef necklace, his rapping wasn't quite as smooth as it had been before.

Kirsty and Rachel were just wondering how they were going to break the news to the goblin that he wasn't going to open the festival after all, when they heard a booming voice. "Who's that rapping *my* words?"

A tall pop star was striding in their direction, wearing a shiny blue suit, an enormous pair of sunglasses and an ice-white baseball cap.

"Jax Tempo!" gulped the goblin rapper, looking terrified. He turned and fled without another word.

"Wait – I thought he was your hero?" Kirsty called in surprise. "Don't you want to meet him?"

Jax Tempo stalked past them towards the rehearsal area. "Nobody's a better rapper than me," they heard him say haughtily.

"Soon I'll be the biggest pop star in the *world*!"

There seemed to be something familiar about him, Rachel thought, but she couldn't put her finger on what it was.

Before she could think about it any more though, she heard an announcement on the backstage tannoy.

"Could The Angels make their way to the main stage, please? The show will begin in two minutes."

Kirsty turned anxiously to Jessie. "I'm glad The Angels will be able to remember their lyrics now that you've got your necklace back, but what about all the other pop star magic? Will they be able to remember their dance steps without Vanessa's magic, and sing properly without Adele's powers?"

"Don't worry," Jessie smiled. "My clef has enough pop star magic to ensure that the whole performance will go smoothly, as long as I stay close to the stage and focus all my strength on the band.

Thanks so much
for helping
me get my
clef necklace
back!"

With a wave
of her wand,
Jessie changed the
girls back into their normal clothes.

"Goodbye, Jessie," Rachel said, smiling
at the little fairy. "That was fun!"

"Goodbye," Kirsty said, as Jessie darted
away towards the stage, like a spark
from a fire. Then the girls hurried around
to the front of the stage and waited
excitedly. A large crowd had gathered
and everyone cheered as the first chords
of *Key to My Heart* sounded and the
three Angels ran on stage.

The Angels looked rather nervous at first but as they launched into the song and got the words and harmonies absolutely perfect, they started to relax and smile.

Rachel and Kirsty were dancing and singing along in the front row. "Look, there's Jessie," Rachel hissed, pointing to where they could just see a dot of twinkling light high above the stage. From the way the dot was wiggling around, it looked as if Jessie was dancing too.

When the song finished, the audience clapped and cheered, then everyone gasped as a puff of rainbow-coloured glitter swirled across the stage. "Just like magic," Rachel heard a girl nearby say, and she exchanged a smile with Kirsty.

Both the friends were pretty certain that the glitter *had* been magic – a last display of fabulous fairy enchantment from Jessie!

"That was awesome," Kirsty sighed happily. "I'm so glad we helped Jessie find her clef in time."

"Me too," Rachel said. "Now we just need to track down the other six magical clefs to make sure the rest of the festival is as good."

"One thing's for sure," Kirsty said.
"It's going to be another exciting holiday
– with fairies, pop music and adventures.
I can't think of anything better!"

**Now Kirsty and Rachel
must help...**

Adele the Singing Coach Fairy

Read on for a sneak peek...

"What a fantastic place for a picnic!"
Rachel Walker exclaimed, her face
breaking into a huge smile.

She and her best friend Kirsty Tate
were standing on a grassy hill above the
site where the Rainspell Island Music
Festival was taking place over five fun-
packed days. Below them the girls could
see the enormous stage surrounded
by lighting rigs and sound equipment.
Close by was Star Village where festival-
goers were able to have a go at being
a pop star themselves. The Village had

a karaoke tent as well as a marquee for dance classes, and there were other areas where people could try out pop star hairstyles and make-up, as well as design their own stage costumes. There were lots of stalls and food tents, too, and a campsite for the festival-goers where Rachel, Kirsty and Rachel's parents were staying.

"OK, girls," called a voice behind them. "The picnic's ready."

Rachel and Kirsty spun around eagerly. Their friends Serena, Lexy and Emilia, otherwise known as the famous pop group The Angels, were sitting on a fluffy pink picnic rug, smiling up at them. Rachel and Kirsty's eyes widened as they saw the three girls surrounded by plates and bowls of delicious food.

"Oh, this looks so glamorous!" Kirsty sighed as she and Rachel joined The Angels on the picnic rug. There were piles of dainty triangular sandwiches scattered with edible glitter, and a crystal glass bowl brimming over with ripe red strawberries alongside another bowl of clotted cream. A jug of freshly-made lemonade with floating ice cubes and slices of lemon stood in the cool shade of a nearby tree...

Read Adele the Singing Coach Fairy to find out what adventures are in store for Kirsty and Rachel!

Meet the
Pop Star Fairies

Kirsty and Rachel have to save Rainspell Island Music Festival after Jack Frost steals the Pop Star Fairies' musical clef necklaces!

www.rainbowmagicbooks.co.uk

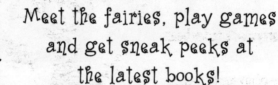

Competition!

Here's a friend who Kirsty and Rachel met in an earlier story. Use the clues below to help you guess her name. When you have enjoyed all seven of the Pop Star Fairies books, arrange the first letters of each mystery fairy's name to make a special word, then send us the answer!

CLUES

1. I love staying overnight with my friends.

2. I carry a cute teddy bear.

3. One of my magic items is a sleeping bag.

The fairy's name is ~~Sheena~~ the ~~sleepover~~ Fairy

We will put all of the correct entries into a draw and select one winner to receive a special Pop Star Fairies goody bag. Your name will also be featured in a forthcoming Rainbow Magic story!

Enter online now at www.rainbowmagicbooks.co.uk

Look out for the next sparkly
Rainbow Magic Special!

Tamara the Tooth Fairy

Kirsty and Rachel must help Tamara the Tooth Fairy get
her three magical items back from Jack Frost. Otherwise,
no tooth will be collected from under your pillow ever again!

Out July 2012